My Senator and Me

A DOG'S-EYE VIEW OF WASHINGTON, D.C.

Senator Edward M. Kennedy

ILLUSTRATED BY DAVID SMALL

SCHOLASTIC INC.
New York Toronto London Auckland
Sydney Mexico City New Delhi Hong Kong

ISBN 978-0-545-24952-2

12 11 10 9 8 7 6 5 4 3 2 1   10 11 12 13 14 15/0

Printed in China   95

This edition first printing, September 2010

The artwork is ink and watercolor.
The type was set in 16-point Schneidler Medium.

This book is a tribute to my Portuguese Water Dog, Splash. Like so many pets in other families, he has added immensely to the joy in our family. Splash is a constant presence in the Capitol and the inspiration for the book. We often meet children in the corridors, and I hope these pages will give them a better understanding of what public service means and how Congress works, and do it in a way that is both appealing and educational. I especially thank my wife Vicki, who has been a strong supporter of this project from the start. She helped immeasurably with this special story and is a wonderful source of support, strength, and love.

E. M. K.

If you want to serve your country, Washington, D.C., is a good place to be. Washington is the capital of the United States. The President lives there. The Supreme Court works there. Congress—made up of the House of Representatives and the Senate—meets there.

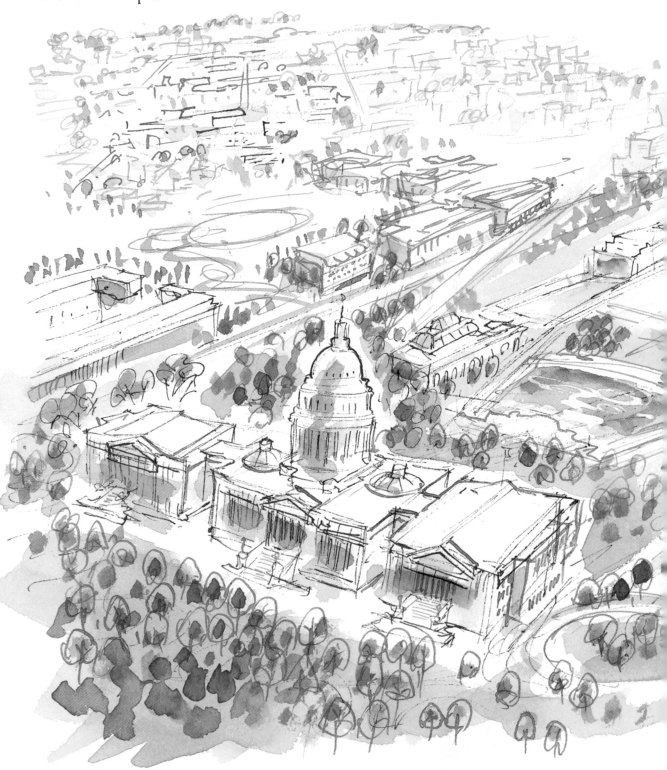

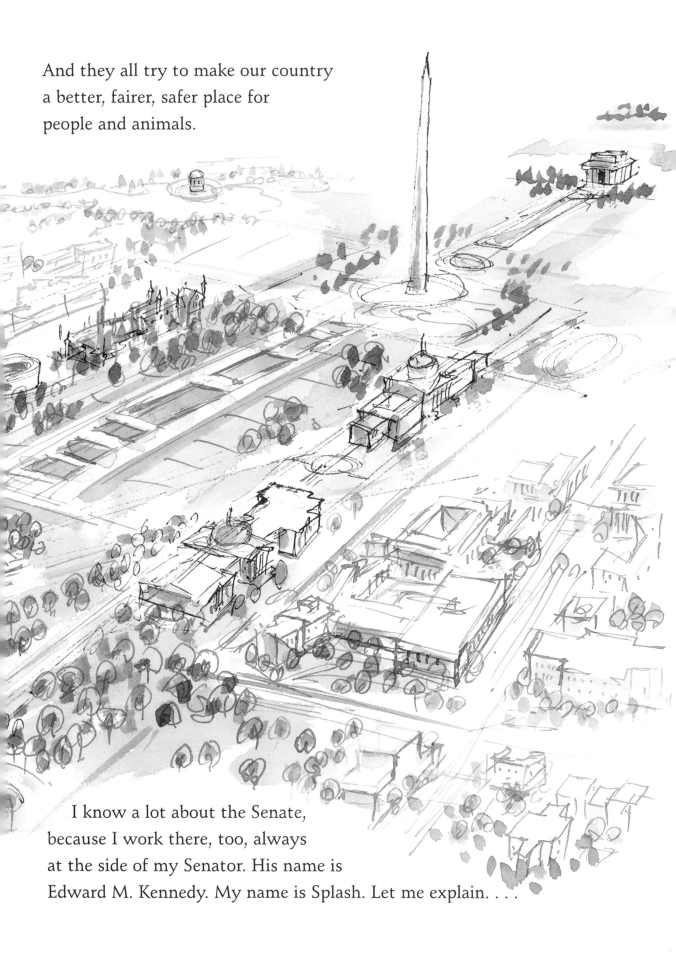

And they all try to make our country
a better, fairer, safer place for
people and animals.

I know a lot about the Senate,
because I work there, too, always
at the side of my Senator. His name is
Edward M. Kennedy. My name is Splash. Let me explain. . . .

The only way to become a Senator is to be elected by the people of your home state. My Senator's home is Massachusetts. It's where he grew up and went to school; it's where he likes to go sailing and spend time with his family. The wonderful people of Massachusetts have elected and reelected him to the Senate for more years than I can even count!

If you are a Senator, you have a lot of responsibility. You probably know hundreds of people. Thousands. Maybe tens of thousands. But are these people your true and loyal friends? There's an old saying: "If you want a friend in Washington, get a dog." A few years ago, my Senator decided to do just that.

My Senator and his wife wanted to find a special dog to become part of their family, so they drove to a farm in Virginia where a family raised Portuguese Water Dogs. Portuguese Water Dogs are strong and smart. They are excellent swimmers and, for centuries, have helped fishermen on their boats. They are very loyal dogs, and they have a lot of love to give.

The Senator and his wife saw many dogs on the farm. Each one had a different personality.

One was rowdy.

One played in the mud.

One liked to sunbathe.

One sat alone.

And one dog stood out from all the others. He was a leader. He walked with confidence and looked after the other dogs. He was very well-behaved, but he also knew how to have fun. His real name was Champion Amigo's Seventh Wave, but because he loved the water, everyone called him "Splash." And that dog was ME!

I walked right up to the Senator and
nuzzled his leg. It was love at first
sight for me—and for him, too. He
rubbed me behind the ears and
admired my curly black coat.
"Feels as soft as a lamb," he said.

We went over to a stretch of grass and played fetch.

"Splash runs like
a champ and never
gives up," my Senator
remarked. "I think I've
found the right dog."

On the drive back to Washington, I sat in the backseat. I couldn't wait to see my new home.

"Look at that, Splash!" My new family talked to me the whole way. They pointed out the White House, where the President lives . . .

. . . the Kennedy Center, where people go to hear music, see plays, and watch the ballet. It was named for my Senator's brother, John F. Kennedy, who was the thirty-fifth President of the United States and a great supporter of the arts . . .

. . . the Lincoln Memorial, where millions of people from all over the world go to remember Abraham Lincoln, the sixteenth President, who led our country during the Civil War . . .

. . . the Washington Monument,
built to honor George Washington,
the first President of the
United States . . .

. . . and finally the Capitol, where Congress meets to decide what's best for the country.

"That's where I work, Splash," my Senator said. "Pretty soon, you'll be going there, too."

It took me a little while to get used to all the traffic and the people in Washington, D.C. But now I know the city like the back of my paw.

A little while ago, we added another
Portuguese Water Dog to our family. Her
name is Sunny, and she's a lot younger
than I am. I'm teaching her everything
she needs to know about Washington.
Every morning at 6:40 A.M., I am the
first one up in the house. I shake
my body, and the tags on my collar
jingle, waking the whole family.

After breakfast, it's time to leave for the office. My Senator and I work at the Russell Senate Office Building, just across the street from the Capitol. To get into the building, everyone has to walk through the metal detector—even me!

When the Capitol Policeman sees me, he grins. "Hi, Splash," he says. I wag my tail to say "hi" back. I love all the attention I get in Washington, but I try not to let that slow me down. My Senator and I have too much to do in a day.

"Let's go to work, Splashie," the Senator says.

At 8:45 sharp, we arrive at the office.

Soon, the Senator's staff comes in for the
morning meeting. Today they are discussing an education bill—that
is, an idea for a new law that will help students and their teachers.

"The Senate has voted to approve our education bill!" one staff
member says. "Our bill will make schools safer, let them hire more
teachers, and even put a computer in every classroom!"

"But the House of Representatives passed a different education
bill," says another staff member. "This is a problem."

"Well, there's no time to lose," says the Senator. "We need to meet with members of the House immediately and work out the differences between the two bills. The schoolchildren are counting on us!"

Suddenly, the Senator's assistant reminds him that he has a press conference in the Capitol at 10 A.M. A press conference in the Capitol means only one thing to me: a ride on the tram! "Let's get moving, Splash," my Senator says in his booming voice.

The tram is an underground train that takes us from the Senate office building to the Capitol. I love every second of the ride: the lurch of the car, the sound of the wheels on the track, the *whoosh* of the air through my fur. My Senator even slips me a liver-flavored treat—my favorite. I am the happiest dog in the world. In less than a minute, the tram arrives at the Capitol.

We go to the press conference on the steps of the Capitol. "We must pass this bill so the children of our country can get the education they deserve," my Senator says.

The crowd nods in agreement. And I sit there, very quietly, looking around to make sure that everything goes well. I know that if I whimper or get up and walk around, someone will whisk me away—away from my Senator—and I won't be invited to any more press conferences.

When the press conference ends, the crowd gathers
around my Senator. Some people reach down to pet me.

After all that hard work, it's time for
a little break. The Senator grins at me.
"Ready to play fetch, boy?"

I am off and running, almost before the words are out of his mouth. He throws a tennis ball high in the air, and I run, run, run to bring it back. I drop the ball at his feet and beg for more. "Woof, woof!" And he throws the ball again and again.

Members of Congress on their way to meetings stop to watch us play. Visitors on their way to libraries and museums watch. Police officers, gardeners, and construction workers taking a break watch us having fun. "Go get 'em, Splash," someone shouts. "Look how high he jumps!" I hear a child say.

We return to the office, where I drink a big bowl of
fresh water and then stretch out on the floor. All
of that exercise makes a dog thirsty—and tired.
My Senator eats lunch at his desk and
prepares for the busy afternoon
ahead. I do not disturb him.

At 2 P.M., we head back to the Capitol for a conference committee meeting.

On the way we see a group of students touring the Capitol with their teacher. I wag my tail and bound over to say "hello." Everybody tries to pet me at once, but I don't mind. The Senator shakes everyone's hand and laughs a lot. The children are from Massachusetts, our home state. Before they leave, we all pose for a group picture.

My Senator and I then walk through
the Capitol rotunda, a beautiful place in
the center of the building. The rotunda is
one of my favorite rooms in the Capitol.

When we arrive at the conference committee session, I make myself comfortable on the floor. I know a meeting like this could go on for hours.

At conference committee meetings, Senators and members of the House of Representatives try to work out the differences between the House and Senate versions of a bill. Today they're discussing my Senator's education bill. Since the bill would improve schools all across the country, I think they should reach a decision quickly and easily. But everyone seems to have their own opinion of the right way to make our schools better, and I wonder whether they'll ever be able to agree.

I listen very carefully to both sides of the debate.

"With all due respect, Senator, we cannot afford this bill."

"I appreciate your concern, Congressman, but we cannot afford *not* to have this bill."

"Congresswoman, our children
are our greatest resource. Therefore,
we need *our* version of the bill."

"Senator, our children are our
greatest resource. Therefore,
we need our version of the bill."

On and on it goes, with one person saying
one thing and another saying the opposite. They
seem to be getting more and more upset, and their
voices are getting louder and louder and louder.

It's time to do something. "WOOF! WOOF!"

They suddenly stop shouting.
The room is completely quiet.
Then my Senator starts to laugh.
And everyone else starts to laugh.
I think they understand what I was getting at.

Working together, cooperating with each other, they finally work out a bill they can agree on.

My Senator leans over and rubs me behind the ears. "Good boy," he whispers. Now the revised bill will be voted on by the Senators and the members of the House of Representatives. And if they agree to pass it, the President of the United States will sign the bill, and we will have a new law to improve our schools. What could be more important than that!

At 4:30, the Senator and I walk over to the Senate reception room. My Senator is going to cast his vote in the Senate chamber, but I have to stay behind. I know the rule: *No dogs allowed on the Senate floor.* But I don't like it. I've seen plenty of Senators, and they don't behave any better than I do!

Voting usually takes the Senators about fifteen minutes.
Fifteen minutes can feel like a very, very long time.

All of a sudden, I hear a familiar
voice and look up at a television set.
My Senator is speaking!

I can't stop my tail—and I don't want to. It's wagging, wagging, wagging as my Senator speaks and then casts his vote. The bill passes, with ninety-five Senators, including mine, voting "yes" and only five voting "no." If I had been allowed to vote, I would have voted "yes," too. Now thousands of schools will be able to give children a better education. And my Senator and I helped make it happen.

At 6:45, we finally leave the office.

We stop on the way home for one more game of fetch.

Back at the house, our family is waiting for us. We eat a delicious dinner. Sunny and I have dog biscuits for dessert.

Then Sunny and I chase each other and play with our toys, while the Senator prepares for the busy day that we are going to have again tomorrow.

It's getting late now. Better get a good night's sleep. Tomorrow's another big day in Washington.

SENATOR EDWARD MOORE KENNEDY

Senator Edward M. Kennedy represented Massachusetts in the United States Senate for forty-seven years, earning himself the nickname "the Lion of the Senate." He was first elected to the Senate in 1962, to finish the term of his brother, John F. Kennedy, who had been elected President in 1960. When Senator Kennedy passed away from brain cancer in August of 2009, he was the third-longest-serving Senator in American history.

Throughout his career, Senator Kennedy fought for issues that benefited the people of Massachusetts and the nation. He and his staff wrote more than three hundred bills that were enacted into law, including many regulations dealing with civil rights, health care, and poverty issues. He served as Chairman of the Health, Education, Labor and Pensions Committee, where he sponsored the creation of the State Children's Health Insurance Program, which provides funds for children's health care. He also served on the Judiciary Committee, the Armed Services Committee, and the Congressional Joint Economic Committee. Outside the Capitol, Senator Kennedy was a founder of the Congressional Friends of Ireland, a founding member of the James Madison Memorial Fellowship Foundation, and a trustee of the John F. Kennedy Center for the Performing Arts.

Senator Kennedy was the youngest of nine children of Joseph P. Kennedy and Rose Fitzgerald Kennedy, and a graduate of Harvard University and the University of Virginia Law School. His wife, Victoria Reggie Kennedy, still lives in their home in Hyannis Port, Massachusetts. The Kennedys have a combined family of five children, Kara, Edward Jr., Patrick, Curran, and Caroline, and four grandchildren, Kiley, Grace, Max, and Teddy III.

SPLASH

Splash's official name is Champion Amigo's Seventh Wave, but his original owner gave him the nickname "Splash." He was born on May 17, 1997. Before he joined the Kennedy family on March 2, 2000, he was a champion show dog in Virginia. In his time on Capitol Hill, he met President Barack Obama, President George W. Bush, President Bill Clinton, and their wives, as well as many other celebrities.

Splash has sailed and swum in Cape Cod, Florida, and the Caribbean. Portuguese Water Dogs have webbed feet to help them swim through the ocean, and they use their tails as a rudder to change directions. When the Kennedy family packs for vacation, Splash sometimes forgets he is a large dog and tries to jump in their suitcases.

Splash loves sailing, swimming, tennis ball fetch, the Special Olympics, and relaxing with the Kennedy family. He dislikes squirrels and people who don't like sailing, swimming, and tennis ball fetch. He lives in Hyannis Port with Victoria Reggie Kennedy, Sunny, and the newest member of the family— another Portuguese Water Dog named Cappy.

HOW A BILL BECOMES A LAW

This book shows part of the process by which a bill becomes a law. If you'd like to know more about that process, it usually happens like this:

1. A senator writes a bill and introduces it to the Senate.

2. The bill is sent to a committee that studies it, talks to experts about it, and sometimes makes changes to it. Once it has the committee's approval, the bill goes back to the Senate.

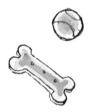

3. All one hundred Senators debate the bill, sometimes making more changes to it in the course of their discussions. Finally, they vote on the bill. If more than half of them vote in favor of it, the bill passes to the other part of Congress, the House of Representatives. (Bills can also originate in the House of Representatives and pass to the Senate.)

4. The House also studies the bill in committee, changes it if necessary, debates it among all four hundred thirty-five representatives, and finally holds a vote on it. If it passes, it then travels to either a conference committee or the President.

5. If there are any differences between the Senate and the House versions of the bill, it goes to a conference committee, where Senators and Representatives work together to resolve the differences between the two versions. (The committee meeting shown in this book is a conference committee meeting.)

6. After everyone has agreed on the revised bill, it returns to the House and the Senate for their final approval. If both houses pass the bill, it is sent to the President.

7. If the President likes the bill, he or she will sign it, and it becomes a law.